Winter Story

A Party In The
Ice Palace

Jill Barklem

PictureLions
An Imprint of HarperCollins*Publishers*

For David

First published in hardback in Great Britain in 1980
First published in paperback in 1995
Text and illustrations copyright © Jill Barklem 1980
A CIP catalogue record for this title is available from the British Library.
The author asserts the moral right to be identified as the author of the work.
ISBN: 0 00 664068 0
Printed and bound in Italy

BRAMBLY HEDGE

For many generations, families of mice have made their homes in the roots and trunks of the trees of Brambly Hedge. If you are ever lucky enough to be nearby, you may see a wisp of smoke from a small chimney or even a steep flight of stairs deep within the trunk of a tree.

Mrs Apple

The mice of Brambly Hedge lead busy lives. They make all their own food and during the fine weather, they collect herbs,

Mr Apple

fruits and nuts from the hedge and surrounding fields. They then prepare delicious jams, pickles and preserves that are kept safely in the Store Stump where Mr Apple is the Warden. Mr Apple's wife, Mrs Apple, is the very best of cooks and their home, Crabapple Cottage, is always filled with the aroma of cakes and freshly baked bread.

Although the mice work hard, they always have time for fun. They welcome the opportunity to meet and celebrate and their favourite place for a party is the Old Oak Palace. This is where Lord and

Primrose

Lady Woodmouse live with their young daughter Primrose.

Lord & Lady Woodmouse

Primrose's best friend is Wilfred Toadflax who lives in the hornbeam tree at the end of the Hedge. Wilfred and his brother Teasel love to play tricks on their sisters Catkin and Clover.

These are just a few of the mice that live in the Hedge. Meet some of their friends and relatives in *Winter Story*.

Wilfred

It was the middle of winter. The sun had just set
and it was very, very cold. An icy wind was blowing
from the East and the wind promised snow.

Deep in the dark roots of Brambly Hedge tiny
lights appeared as lamps were lit in the windows.

More little lights could be seen leaving the Store
Stump, moving hastily along the hedgerow and
disappearing into holes hidden in the twisty roots.
The mice had smelled snow in the air and were
all hurrying home to a nice hot supper by the fire.

Mr Apple, warden of the Store Stump, was the last to leave for home. By the time he reached Crabapple Cottage, the first flakes were beginning to fall.

"Is that you, dear?" called Mrs Apple as he let himself in through the front door. Delicious smells wafted down from the kitchen. Mrs Apple had spent the afternoon baking pies, cakes and puddings for the cold days to come. She drew two armchairs up to the fire and brought in their supper on a tray.

There was a lot of noise coming from the hornbeam
tree next door. The Toadflax children had never seen
snow before.

"It's snowing! It really is SNOWING!" squeaked the
two boys, Wilfred and Teasel. They chased their sisters

Clover and Catkin round the kitchen, with pawfuls of
snow scooped from the windowsill.

"Suppertime!" called Mrs Toadflax firmly, ladling hot
chestnut soup into four small bowls.

After supper the children were sent off to bed,
but they were far too excited to sleep. As soon as
the grown-ups were safely occupied downstairs,
they climbed out of their bunk beds to watch the
snowflakes falling past the window.

"Tobogganing tomorrow," said Wilfred.

"Snow pancakes for tea," said Clover.

"We'll make a snow mouse," said Catkin.

"And I'll knock it down!" said Teasel, pushing the
girls off their chair.

Next morning the mice along the hedgerow woke to
find their windows half-blocked by snow. Mrs Apple
had to stand on tiptoes on the kitchen table to see out.

And what a sight met her eyes! The fields were covered with a thick, white blanket of snow and all the paths and plants had disappeared beneath it.

When the Toadflax family went down to breakfast, they found the kitchen dark and still. Mrs Toadflax put fresh wood on the fire and set Clover to work with the toasting fork. Soon they were all sitting round the table, eating hot buttered toast, drinking blackberry leaf tea and making plans for the day ahead.

The snow was thicker than the mice had expected.
All the downstairs windows along the hedgerow were
covered with snow and many of the upper ones, too,
were hidden in deep drifts.

The mice leaned out of their bedroom windows to
wave and call to their friends.

"Enough for a Snow Ball, wouldn't you say?" called
Toadflax to Mrs Apple.

"A Snow Ball!" echoed the little mice, gleefully.

Every family along the hedgerow kept shovels, maps and ropes in a special cupboard by the front door and after breakfast the mice dug tunnels from tree to tree, linking them all to the Store Stump. Teasel and Wilfred were sent down to help, but they soon found that it was much more fun to throw snow at each other and so were sent home again.

Lord Woodmouse dug his way through to old
Mrs Eyebright and helped her to light a fire.

"I haven't seen snow like this since I was young,"
she sighed. "The last Snow Ball was held in the
year Mr Eyebright and I were married. I'm the
only one left who can remember it now."

When the tunnels were finished, all the mice
gathered noisily in the Store Stump Hall.

Mrs Apple took some seed cake from the cupboard and prepared a jug of acorn coffee. The mice helped themselves and gathered round Mr Apple, who held up a paw for silence.

"Lord Woodmouse and I have agreed," he said when they were quiet, "that we should follow in the tradition of our forefathers." He cleared his throat nervously, straightened his whiskers, and recited,

> "*When the snows are lying deep,*
> *When the field has gone to sleep,*
> *When the blackthorn turns to white,*
> *And frosty stars bejewel the night,*
> *When summer streams are turned to ice,*
> *A Snow Ball warms the hearts of mice.*

"Friends, I declare that a Snow Ball will take place at dusk tonight in the Ice Hall."

"Where's that?" whispered Clover, as the mice clapped and cheered.

"Wait and see!" replied Mrs Apple. "You come home with me and help prepare the feast."

There was a deep drift of snow banked against the Store Stump and the elder mice, after discussion, declared it to be "just right" for the Ice Hall. Mr Apple dug the first tunnel to check that the snow was firm.

"It's perfect!" he called back from the middle of the drift. The mice picked up their shovels and the digging began.

The snow was dug from inside the drift, piled into carts and taken down to the stream. Wilfred and Teasel helped enthusiastically, but they were sent home again when Mr Apple caught them putting icicles down Catkin's dress.

The middle of the drift was carefully hollowed out. Mr Apple inspected the roof very thoroughly to make sure that it was safe.

"Safe as the Store Stump!" he declared.

All the kitchens along Brambly Hedge were
warm and busy. Hot soups, punches and puddings
bubbled and in the ovens pies browned and sizzled.
Clover and Catkin helped Mrs Apple string

crabapples to roast over the fire. The boys had
to sit and watch because they ate too many.

"It's not that I mind, dears, but we must have SOME
left for the punch!"

The Glow-worms were put in charge of the lighting. Toadflax fetched them early from the bank at the end of the Hedge, for Mrs Apple had insisted that they should have a good supper before their long night's work began.

By tea-time the Hall was finished. The ice columns and carvings sparkled in the blue-green light and the polished dance floor shone. Tables were set at the end of the Hall and eager cooks bustled in from their kitchens with baskets of food.

The children decorated a small raised platform with sprays of holly, while Basil, the keeper of the hedgerow wines, set out some chairs for the musicians.

When all was done, the mice admired their handiwork and went home to wash and change.

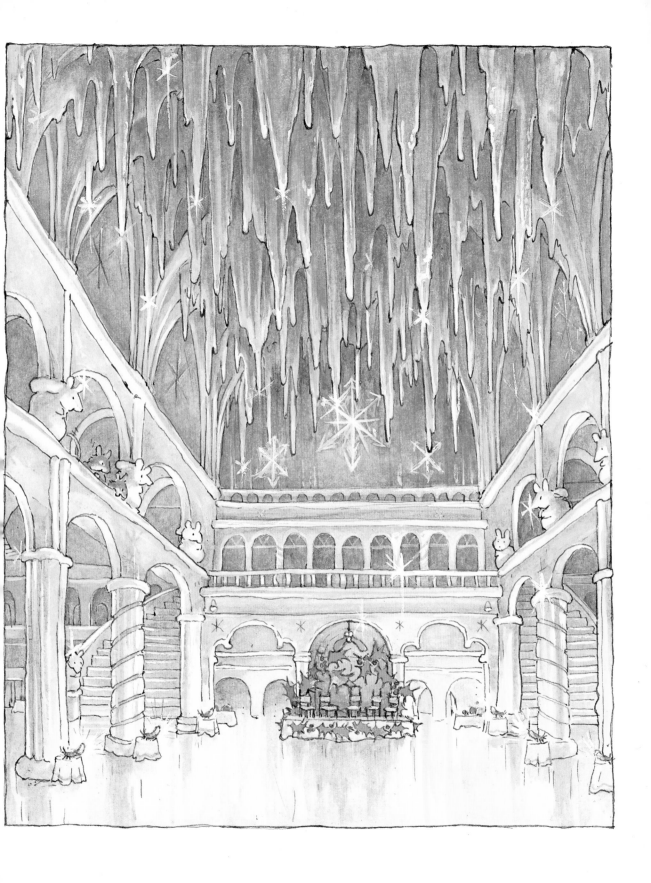

As muffs and mufflers were left at the door, it was clear that all the mice had dressed up for the grand occasion. Wilfred and Teasel crept under a table to watch and every now and then a little paw appeared and a cream cake disappeared.

Basil struck up a jolly tune on his violin and the
dancing began. All the dances were very fast and twirly
and were made even faster by the slippery ice floor.
Wilfred and Teasel whirled their sisters round so quickly
that their paws left the ground.

"I don't feel very well," said Clover, looking rather green.

Mrs Apple stood on a chair and banged two saucepan lids together.

"Supper is served," she called.

The eating and drinking and dancing carried on late into the night. At midnight, all the hedgerow children were taken home to bed.

As soon as they were safely tucked up, their parents
returned to the Ball. Basil made some hot blackberry
punch and the dancing got faster and faster.

The Snow Ball went on until dawn.

The musicians were tired. The ice columns began
to drip. The sleepy mice could dance no more. They
wandered home through the snow tunnels, climbed
the stairs and crept into their warm beds.

Outside the window, the snow had started to fall again.
But every mouse in Brambly Hedge was fast asleep.